FAME THING

JONATHAN MERES

With illustrations by

JAKE McDONALD

Barrington Stoke

To Aidan — snowboarding superstar!

First published in 2006 in Great Britain by
Barrington Stoke Ltd
18 Walker Street, Edinburgh, EH3 7LP

www.barringtonstoke.co.uk

This edition first published 2016

Text © 2006 Jonathan Meres
Illustrations © 2016 Jake McDonald

The moral right of Jonathan Meres and Jake McDonald to be
identified as the author and illustrator of this work has been
asserted in accordance with the Copyright, Designs and Patents
Act, 1988

A CIP catalogue record for this book is available
from the British Library upon request

ISBN: 978-1-78112-679-0

Printed in China by Leo

CONTENTS

CHAPTER 1
NAME THING

The school bus drove off. George and her brother Denis were all alone. It was a warm spring afternoon. Birds sang in the trees. The old church clock struck four. But George had only one thing on her mind.

"Well?" she said.

"Well what?" said Denis.

"Who do you think's going to win tonight?"

Denis let out a long sigh. "I have no idea who's going to win tonight, George. And do you know something? I couldn't care less."

George looked up at Denis from her wheelchair. "Are you serious?"

"I've never been more serious in my life," said Denis.

"No, but really."

"No, but really, George. I couldn't care less."

"But it's the semi-final replay, Den! You've got to care!"

"Have I?" said Denis. "Why's that then?"

"Because ... because ..." George said. "Because you just have to, that's all!"

Denis laughed.

"What's so funny?"

"You, George. You're funny."

"I don't see what's so funny about liking football," muttered George.

"*Liking* football?" Denis said. "You're obsessed with it! Football's all you ever think about!"

"So?" George said. "What's wrong with that?"

Denis rolled his eyes. She just didn't get it, did she? She just couldn't get her head round the fact that he'd sooner watch paint dry than watch a football match.

"Oh, I don't know," he said. "Everything?"

"Anyway, it's not my fault," George went on.

"Really?" said Denis, sounding surprised. "So whose fault is it, then?"

"Dad's," George said.

"Dad's?" Denis looked at his sister. "How do you work that out then?"

"Well, he's the one who named me after a famous footballer, isn't he?"

"He named me after a famous footballer as well," Denis said. "And I hate football."

Denis didn't like anyone to know why he was called Denis. He'd been named after Denis Law, who'd played for Manchester United back in the 60s. His sister George was named after George Best, another old United player and one of the

4

most famous footballers ever. Her proper name wasn't really George, though – it was Georgina. But everyone called her George.

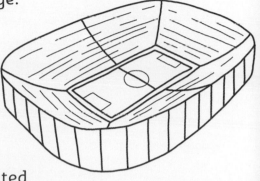

"So?" said George.

Denis didn't say anything, as he started to push his sister along the pavement. If she wanted to have the last word, he thought, then fine, she could have the last word.

"Get a move on!" George said. "I can go faster than this myself!"

But Denis just smiled. He knew she was kidding.

"Oi, Georgie!" a voice yelled from across the road.

George turned around. It was her best friend Nick's dad.

"What's the score going to be tonight then?" he shouted.

Denis shook his head. What was it with these people? Hadn't they got better things to think about?

"3–1 to Chelsea," George yelled. "After extra time."

"What?" Denis said. "So now you can predict the future?"

George didn't reply. She'd spotted a huge removals lorry as it roared past them and rumbled round the corner.

"Did you see that?" she said.

"Yeah," Denis said. "A lorry. What about it?"

"Not just any lorry," said George. "A removals lorry,"

"So?" said Denis.

"It must be going to The Elms."

"Great," said Denis, trying not to yawn.

"I wonder who it is then?" George said. "They reckon it might be someone famous."

"Dunno," said Denis. "You tell me. You're the one with special powers."

"Ha ha," George said. "Very funny."

"You don't mean that, do you?" said Denis.

"What do you think?" said George.

CHAPTER 2

YOU'RE KIDDING!

It had been the talk of the village for months. Who was going to move into The Elms?

The Elms was the biggest house for miles around. It had a swimming pool and a tennis court, as well as huge sweeping lawns and a lake.

The house itself was very old. It had at least ten bedrooms. And there was a library and a ballroom and a hall full of suits of armour.

Ever since the "For Sale" sign had been taken down and the "Sold" sign had gone up, all anyone wanted to talk about was – *Who has bought The Elms?*

Some people said it was someone famous, like a pop star. Or maybe an actor.

There were some people in the village who said they didn't want any showbiz types moving in. Others thought it would be brilliant. After all, this was a place where the closest thing to a celebrity was some guy who'd been an extra in a soap opera.

"I think they should turn it into something useful, like an old folks' home," said George's mum, as she sat down to have tea with George and Denis.

"So do I, Mum," Denis said. "There's something wrong about just one person living in a place that big when homeless people are living on the streets."

"How do you know it's just one person?" said George. "And anyway, are you telling me you wouldn't buy a place like that if you could afford it?"

"Correct," Denis said.

"You liar!"

"Come on you two, stop it now," Mum said.

"Have you got a cloth, Mum?" said George.

"A cloth?" said Mum. "What for?"

"To polish Denis's halo."

"Grow up, George," Denis said.

But before George could reply, her mobile rang.

"Hello," she said. "Hi, Nick, how's it going?" She paused. "You're kidding!"

Denis and his mum looked at each other. Why was George's best friend ringing? What could have happened?

"You have *got* to be kidding!" George screeched into her phone.

"What is it?" Denis said, but George just ignored him.

"If this is your idea of a joke, Nick Watson, I'm going to ..."

But then George stopped talking and listened.

"You've seen him?" she said.

"Who?" Denis said.

"Are you sure it was him?" said George.

"Who?" Denis and Mum yelled together.

"I'll be round in two minutes!" said George, ignoring her mum and her brother. "Yeah. Bye!" And with that, George put her phone back in her pocket.

"You're never going to guess who's moved into The Elms," she said.

"You're right. We never are, so why don't you just tell us?" Denis said.

"Only Dean flipping Johnson, that's who!"

"Dean Johnson?" Mum said. "You mean the footballer?"

George looked at her mum as if she'd just stepped off a spaceship.

"There's only one Dean Johnson, Mum. Of course I mean the footballer!"

"He's very young, isn't he?" Mum said.

"Yeah," Denis said. "And very stupid."

"You're just jealous," George said.

"What? Jealous of a guy with a brain the size of a snail's?" Denis said. "I don't think so!"

"For someone who hates football, you know an awful lot about it," said George.

"Dean Johnson's never out of the news!" said Denis. "Everyone knows about him. There's a different story every day!"

"Aren't you supposed to be going round to Nick's, George?" said her mum, changing the subject before a fight broke out.

"Do you mind, Mum?"

"Do I have a choice?" Mum asked.

"Not really, no," George said, breaking into a grin.

"Go on, then."

"Thanks, Mum."

There was a moment's pause. George looked at her brother and smiled. "Denis?"

Denis knew what she was going to ask.

"Any chance of a push?" George said.

"I thought you said you can go faster by yourself?"

"Pleeeeeeeease?" said George in a girly voice.

Denis looked at his mum.

"Go on. Clear off, the pair of you." She sighed. "You can have your tea when you get back."

"Thanks, Mum," Denis said.

"I owe you one, Den," George said.

"You owe me more than one."

George smiled.

"That was rotten, what you said just then," she said to Denis when they got outside.

"What? You mean about Dean Johnson having a brain the size of a snail's?" said Denis.

"It was offensive."

"Yeah," said Denis. "Offensive to snails."

"Idiot," said George.

"Love you, too." Denis laughed.

CHAPTER 3

THE BOY WITH THE GOLDEN FEET

Dean Johnson hadn't even turned 17 when he became the youngest ever player to score a goal in the Premier League. And what a goal it had been. An absolute screamer from the edge of the box. The goalie didn't get anywhere near it. The crowd went crazy. Right there, right then, a star was born.

Dean proved he wasn't just a one-hit wonder when he scored another goal in the next match. In fact, he scored five goals in his first seven games.

And they were all screamers. Volleys, long-range shots, diving headers, the lot! Dean didn't seem to score ordinary goals. He left those to ordinary players.

A buzz went through the crowd whenever Dean got the ball. They always expected him to score, or at the very least, do something exciting. And Dean hardly ever disappointed. More often than not, he delivered the goods. The fans chanted his name. He was the new football god.

Dean didn't seem like he was the smartest guy on the block. People said he wasn't what you'd call rocket scientist material. But that didn't bother Dean. He didn't want to be a rocket scientist. The only thing he'd ever wanted to do was play football. And, boy, could Dean Johnson play football!

The whole world went Dean crazy. The papers all called him "Deano". It was *Deano* this, *Deano* that and *Deano* the other. It seemed that Dean could do no wrong. No one had a bad word to say about him. Kids loved him. Mums and dads loved him. Grandmas and Grandpas loved him. Everybody loved him.

And everyone agreed. Dean Johnson was the Boy with the Golden Feet.

He wasn't what you'd call super-handsome. In fact, he was really quite ordinary looking. But that didn't stop him from appearing in loads of adverts. Before long his face was being used to sell everything, from hair gel to soft drinks and crisps.

Dean soon became very rich indeed. He had more money than he knew what to do with. More money than sense, some people said. But Dean didn't care. He bought his first Ferrari when he was still too young to drive it. He bought his second one just after that.

So Dean spent the next few months being the centre of attention and loving every minute of it. He went to all the best shows and all the most glitzy showbiz parties. He hung out with rock stars, film stars and even politicians. And the weird thing was, they all wanted to be seen with Dean, not the other way round.

And then it happened. A row in a club. Jealous boys and crying girls. Raised voices and raised fists. A scuffle. Punches thrown.

A photographer from a newspaper just happened to be there. Some people said it was all a set-up. That it was too much of a coincidence. That the people involved had been offered money.

Whatever the truth was, the punch-up led to Dean Johnson's first ever bit of bad press.

"DANCING DEANO SHOWN RED CARD!" the headline screamed, above a photo of Dean being thrown out of the club.

There were plenty more bad headlines after that night.

"DEANO ROYALE!" said one, when Dean was pictured stumbling out of a casino in the early hours of the morning.

"DEANO DECKS DAVE!" said another, after a fan claimed Dean had hit him just because he'd asked for a selfie.

And just like that, the tide had turned. It was the end of Dean Johnson's all-too-short honeymoon with an adoring public. He was no longer the Boy with the Golden Feet. No, Deano was now a wild, foul-mouthed, overpaid idiot.

Everyone agreed. Dean Johnson had grown too big for his golden boots.

CHAPTER 4

QUESTION TIME

George started asking questions before Nick had even opened the door.

"So, what's he like then? Did you say anything to him? Did he see you? Did he say anything to you? What's he like? Come on! I'm waiting!"

George stopped, but only because she'd run out of breath. Nick thought for a moment.

"OK, for a start, no, I don't know what he's like," he said. "No, I didn't say anything to him, and no, he didn't say anything to me."

Nick paused.

"Oh and I don't know if he saw me because he just drove right past. He might have done. But I'm not sure. Amazing car by the way. Red Ferrari! Convertible!"

"Hi, Nick," Denis said.

"Hi, Denis," Nick replied.

"Look, I'd love to stop, I really would," Denis said, as he began to head back down the path. "Except I already have a life, thanks."

"Hey, look, you might not think this is a big deal," George shouted after him. "But it is! It's a huge deal!"

Denis shrugged. "Whatever," he said.

"Don't give me that 'whatever' rubbish, Den," said George. "*Whatever* is what people say when they know they're wrong!"

Denis shrugged again. "Whatever," he said, setting off down the street.

George thought about yelling something else, but didn't. There were more important matters to attend to.

"So are we going to go round there or what, then?" she said.

"What? You mean and just hang around outside the gates like a couple of saddos?" said Nick.

"Exactly," said George.

"Sounds good to me," Nick said.

"Excellent," George said. "Let's go!"

The questions began again the moment they set off.

"So what did he look like?" George asked.

"Just like he looks on the telly," said Nick.

"Did he have anyone with him?"

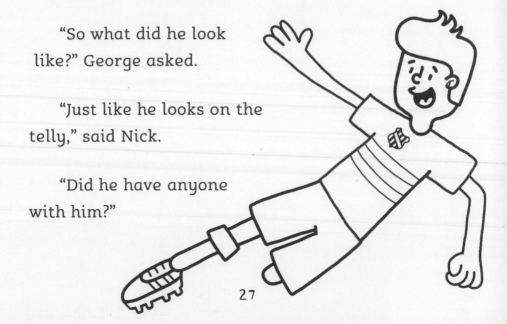

"Like who?" Nick said.

"Like a girl or anything?" George said.

"I don't think so, no. Why?"

"Nothing," said George. "No reason. I just wondered, that's all."

Nick didn't say anything, but when George turned to look at him, she could see he was smiling.

"What's the matter?" George said.

"You fancy him, don't you?"

"Eh? What are you on about? Course I don't!"

"So how come you've gone red?"

"I've not gone red!" George protested. But she knew that she had.

"You fancy him. I know you do!" teased Nick.

"I do not!"

Nick just smiled again.

"Stop smiling like that!"

"Like what?"

"Like that!"

Nick might have been George's best friend, but sometimes he drove her mad. This was one of those sometimes.

"It's OK if you do fancy him, George," he said.

"I didn't realise I needed your permission," said George. "But thanks anyway."

"But ..."

"But nothing!" said George. "I don't fancy him."

"Yeah, but I'm just saying that if you did ..."

"Nick?"

"Yeah?"

"I do NOT fancy Dean Johnson!" George yelled. "Which part of that don't you understand?"

"OK, OK!"

"And even if I did ... which I don't ... he's not going to go out with me, is he? I mean, do I look like a footballer's girlfriend?"

"Er, not really, no," said Nick.

"Well then," George said. "I'm hurt, Nick, I really am. You think I'd fancy somebody just because they're famous and they've got loads of money? What do you take me for?"

"Sorry," said Nick.

"I should think so too," said George.

By now they'd arrived outside The Elms. Workers were busy fitting electronic gates and CCTV cameras.

"Are those to help keep us out, or him in?" George asked.

Nick laughed. "What d'you think he's really like? Do you think all that stuff in the papers is true?"

"Why don't you ask him?" said a voice.

George and Nick turned round.

It was Dean Johnson.

CHAPTER 5

WHEN GEORGE MET DEAN

George couldn't help screaming. It was just such a shock to see one of her heroes standing there.

She'd seen him on TV millions of times, of course. But this was different. He was right in front of her.

"Sorry," Dean said. "I didn't mean to scare you."

"That's OK," George croaked.

"I'm Dean, by the way," he went on.

"I know you are," George said.

"What's your name?"

"Erm ..."

George was still in shock.

"Her name's George," said Nick. "After George Best."

"Georgie Best, eh?" said Dean. "He was some player."

"I'm Nick, by the way."

"Pleased to meet you, Nick," said Dean.

Nick and Dean shook hands.

"Pleased to meet you too, George," said Dean, holding out his hand.

"Pleased to meet you," George just about managed to say, taking Dean's hand and shaking it.

"Right, well, that's the formal stuff over with," said Dean. "Are you coming in or what?"

"Sorry?" George said.

Had she heard right? Was Dean Johnson really inviting them into his home? He couldn't be! He was one of the most famous people in the country! Why would he do a thing like that? It had to be some kind of mistake.

But it wasn't.

"I thought you might like to come in or something?" said Dean. "Everything's still in boxes.

But the TV's unpacked. And the match is about to start. I want to know who we're going to play in the Final. You don't have to if you don't want to. But ..."

Dean never got to finish his sentence. Nick was already pushing George up the drive.

"I'll take that as a 'yes' then." Dean laughed, following them.

"What are you doing?" hissed George.

"What does it look like I'm doing?" said Nick.

"We can't do this!"

"We flipping well can!" said Nick.

"But he's a complete stranger!"

"No, he's not! He's Dean Johnson!"

"Yes," said George. "But ..."

"So what's this place like then?" said Dean, catching up with them.

"Oh, er, quiet," said George. "Very quiet."

"That's good," said Dean.

"You must have known that, though?"

"What?" Dean said. "Nah, not really. It's the first time I've been here."

"Are you serious?" said Nick.

"Yeah."

"How come?"

"Everything gets done for me," said Dean. "About the only thing I have to do myself is wipe my own bum. And I'm pretty sure if I asked, they'd do that for me too."

"Who's 'they'?" said George.

"My people," said Dean.

"Your people? You sound like Jesus or something."

"Jesus? Who does he play for?"

George hoped Dean was joking. He couldn't be that stupid, could he?

"What kind of people?" asked Nick.

"Agents, PR people, that kind of thing," said Dean. "There's loads of them."

"What do PR people do?" Nick asked.

"Good question," said Dean. "Not much, if you ask me. I should sack the lot of them."

"PR means Public Relations," George explained. "They deal with the press and all that."

By now they were at the house. The lorry George had spotted before was outside and the removal men were running up and down a wooden ramp, like busy worker ants.

Nick started to push George up the ramp and towards the house. But it proved to be hard work.

"Come on, Nick!" George teased. "I thought boys were supposed to be stronger than girls!"

"Shut your face, you!" said Nick. "If you weren't such a porker –!"

"A porker?" George laughed. "How dare you?"

"Here, let me," said Dean, taking over from Nick.

"Thanks," said George.

"Does your boyfriend always talk to you like that?" Dean asked.

"Nick?" George was horrified. "My boyfriend? Are you crazy?"

"Oi!" said Nick, pretending to be upset.

"Haven't you got a boyfriend, then?" asked Dean.

"No," George said. "Why? Have you got a girlfriend?"

"Depends," said Dean.

"On what?" George said.

"Which paper you read."

George smiled. She suspected that Dean Johnson might not be so stupid after all.

CHAPTER 6
FAME THING

The Elms was every bit as grand on the inside as it looked from the outside.

"Well? What do you think?" said Dean.

"It's amazing!" said Nick. "You could fit the whole of my house into this hall!"

"Yeah, same here," said Dean. "Well, the house I used to live in, anyway."

"It's ridiculous," George said.

"George!" Nick hissed.

"No, she's right," said Dean. "It *is* ridiculous. Anyone fancy a drink, by the way? I could murder a Coke."

"Yeah, that would be great, thanks," said George.

"Excuse me, mate," Dean said to a removal man. "Which way is it to the kitchen?"

"Straight on past the dining room, along the corridor and it's first on the right. You can't miss it."

"Cheers, mate," said Dean.

Nick was amazed. "You mean you've not even been to your own kitchen yet?"

"I've been," said Dean. "I just can't remember how to get there."

"This place is unreal," said George.

"My whole life is unreal." Dean chuckled. "Come on, let's go."

They set off together.

"So, who do you fancy then?" said Dean.

"Pardon?" George said.

"Who do you fancy?" Dean repeated. "To win tonight?"

"Oh, I see," George said. "Erm, Chelsea. 3–1 after extra time. How about you?"

"Yeah, Chelsea. 2–0," said Dean.

"And what about the Final?" George said. "Do you think you'll win?"

Dean smiled. "Do you want a Coke or not?" he said.

"Yeah, shut up, George!" said Nick. "I think you'll win, Dean. No problem."

"Cheers, mate. I hope you're right," said Dean. "Hey, look, we've made it!"

They were in the kitchen. It was huge. Just like everything else in the house. Dean headed for the fridge, opened the door and took out three cans of Coke.

"Here you go." He handed a can each to George and Nick.

"This is crazy," said George.

"What is?" said Dean.

"Us being here," said George. "With you."

"What's so crazy about that?" Dean said.

"You're Dean Johnson!"

"Yeah, I know I am," said Dean. "So what?"

"You're famous!"

"Does that mean I'm only allowed to hang out with other famous people?"

Dean was smiling, but George had a feeling that he wasn't joking.

"I never asked to be famous, you know," Dean went on. "All I wanted to do was play football. It's my job. A job I happen to get paid shedloads of money for doing. I'm just lucky. I mean, look at this place! I don't belong here! I'm just a normal bloke! This time last year I was still living in a council house with my mum!"

"Sorry," said George.

"Why?" Dean said, smiling. "What's wrong with my mum?"

"No, I meant sorry about the fame thing," said George. "It must be hard."

"It is," Dean said. "Or it can be. I mean, don't get me wrong. Sometimes it can be great. But other times it can be a pain in the backside."

They all took another gulp of Coke.

"I shouldn't even be drinking this stuff," said Dean, patting his stomach. "Got to watch the sugar intake."

"Oh, I don't know," said George. "You look all right to me."

48

Nick sniggered.

"What?" George snapped.

"Nothing," said Nick.

But at that moment a phone rang. It was Dean's mobile.

"Hello?" he said, answering it. "Oh hi, Jeff. Where are you?"

"Right behind you," said a voice.

They all spun round to see who it was.

Standing in the doorway of the kitchen was a guy wearing an expensive suit and an even more expensive tan. He had long, slicked-back hair and was grinning from ear to ear.

"Just thought I'd come and see how my boy was doing," he said.

"I'm doing fine, thanks, Jeff," said Dean.

"That's good, that's good," said the guy.

He looked at Nick and then down at George, sitting in her wheelchair.

"Well? Are you going to introduce me to your friends, or what?"

"Oh yeah, sorry," said Dean. "This is Nick, this is George. Guys, this is my agent, Jeff Edwards."

"Hi," Jeff said. He held his hand out towards Nick.

Nick shook it. "Hi," he said.

Jeff turned to George and bent down so that he was at her level.

"Hell-ooo!" he said in a slow, loud voice. "How are yooooooou todaaaaay?"

George looked at him. This guy was talking to her like she was a baby. Or deaf. Or stupid. Or all three.

"I'm oo-kaaaaay thank yoooooou!!!" George shouted back.

If Jeff Edwards wanted to treat her like an idiot, that was fine by George. She thought he was an idiot too.

CHAPTER 7
THE MAGIC NUMBER

George opened her eyes. Sunlight was streaming through the curtains. She could hear voices downstairs. It sounded like her mum and dad were having breakfast. Along the corridor the toilet flushed. A few moments later there was a bang on the door.

"You awake yet, George?" Denis said.

"No!"

"OK," said Denis. "Let me know when you are. I'll give you a hand down the stairs."

"OK," George said. "Thanks."

George lay in bed, thinking about the night before. Had she really met Dean Johnson? Had she really sat in his house, drinking Coke and watching the match? It seemed like a dream. Perhaps it *was* a dream.

George turned to look at the clock next to her bed. There was a scrap of paper with a phone number scribbled on it. So it was true. George hadn't been dreaming after all. It really had happened.

"Give me a call some time," Dean had said. "We could hang out."

George smiled to herself. Dean Johnson? Wanting to hang out? With her? It was incredible!

She looked at the scrap of paper again. There were people at school who'd do anything to get their hands on that number. She could make an absolute fortune if she wanted to.

George switched her phone on. She added Dean's number to her contacts, then threw the bit of paper away.

George knew that this was something she was going to keep to herself. She wasn't going to tell anyone that she had Dean Johnson's number. She wasn't even going to tell anyone she'd met him. This time yesterday, George would have boasted and bragged about meeting Dean Johnson. But not now. Not any more. Something had changed.

George's mum and dad were already having breakfast, when she entered the kitchen.

"Well? What was he like?" said George's dad, before his daughter had even got to the table.

"Morning, Dad," George said.

"Never mind morning," he said. "We're waiting!"

"Speak for yourself, Dad," said Denis, as he helped himself to a bowl of cereal.

"Oh come on, Den. Don't tell me you're not interested!"

"OK, I won't then," Denis said.

"I think you might be surprised, Den," George said. She took a slice of toast.

"Oh yeah?" Denis said. "Come on then, George. Surprise me."

George thought for a moment.

"Nah, I don't think so," she said.

George's dad looked at her as if she'd gone mad. She hadn't wanted to speak about it when she'd got back the night before either. What was wrong? George was even more football crazy than he was!

"So is that it, then?" Dad asked.

"What do you mean? *Is that it?*" George said.

"Is that all you've got to say?"

"Er, yeah. 'Fraid so. Sorry."

"That's not fair!" said her dad.

"Leave her alone," said her mum. "She doesn't want to talk about it. Can't you tell?"

"I only wanted to know what he's like in real life," Dad said in a sulky voice.

"Time to get going," Mum said, glancing up at the clock. "You don't want to be late for school."

"Ah well, you see, that's where you're wrong, Mum," Denis said. "I'd love to be late for school. How about you, George?"

But George didn't reply. She'd just remembered. Her best friend, Nick. Nick, who couldn't keep his mouth shut if you paid him to. Nick, who couldn't keep a secret if his life depended on it. Nick, who would want to tell the whole world about meeting Dean Johnson.

"Oh, no," she groaned.

"What's the matter, love?" her mum asked.

"Nothing, Mum."

CHAPTER 8

TO TEXT OR NOT TO TEXT?

George sat on the school bus and stared out of the window. She thought about the scrap of paper. The scrap of paper with Dean Johnson's number on it!

Was Dean serious when he told George to call him? Perhaps he was just saying that. Perhaps he was just being nice. Perhaps it wasn't even his real number.

There was only one way to find out. George took her phone out of her pocket.

She thought it was better to text. That way it wouldn't be so embarrassing if it wasn't Dean's real number after all.

She looked at her phone. What should she say? She'd only ever texted mates before. She'd certainly never texted anyone famous.

But then George remembered what Dean had said about the whole fame thing. About how hard it was. About how he just wanted to be normal.

In the end George thought she'd keep things simple. She typed –

Hi. Thanks for the Coke! Good luck in the Final! George :)

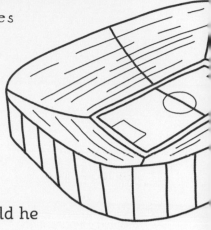

George looked at the
text for a few moments.
Should she send it or not?
After all, Dean must get
hundreds of messages a day!
Would he bother to reply? Would he
even remember who she was?

'Oh, what the heck,' thought George as she added
Dean's number.

"Dean? Who's Dean?"

George turned around. Amy Chan was peering
over the back of her seat.

"Oh, just some guy," said George.

"Well – *duh*," said Amy. "Come on, George, who
is he?"

"None of your business!" said George.

"Ooooh!" said Amy. "Pardon me for breathing!"

George pressed "send" and put her phone away.

"What's he like?" said Amy. "Is he fit?"

"Depends what kind of 'fit' you mean," Nick said, as he came and sat down next to George.

"What do you mean?" said Amy.

"I mean," said Nick, "are we talking 'fit' as in good looking, or 'fit' as in being able to run round for 90 minutes?"

"What are you on about?" said Amy.

"Yes, Nick, what are you on about?" George hissed.

Nick looked at George. Why was she staring at him like that? What was the problem? He didn't understand.

"You haven't told her then, George?" he asked.

"Told me what?" said Amy.

"About where we were last night," said Nick.

"Why?" said Amy. "Where were you?"

George sighed. There was no point trying to stop Nick now. He was bound to blab sooner or later. It looked like it was going to be sooner.

"You're never going to believe it," he said.

"Try me," said Amy.

"I'm telling you," said Nick. "You won't believe it."

"If you must know, we were at Dean Johnson's place!" said George.

In an instant, Amy's smile vanished.

"Dean Johnson?" she said. "The footballer?"

"No," said George. "Dean Johnson the painter and decorator."

Amy smiled. "Really? You were at Dean Johnson's place?" she said. "Yeah, right."

"OK, we weren't, then," said George.

"I told you you wouldn't believe it," said Nick.

"I wouldn't have believed it myself this time yesterday," George said.

Amy looked at George. "You really were at Dean Johnson's place?"

"We really were," said George.

"That's who's bought The Elms," Nick chipped in.

"This is a wind-up," said Amy. "I know it is."

"It's not," said Nick. "It's the truth. Honest."

At that moment, George's phone rang. She looked at it. "Oh my God! It's him!" she screeched.

"Who?" Nick asked.

"Who do you think? Dean!"

"Aaaaaaggghhhh!!!!" Amy screamed.

"Shut up!" George hissed. "I don't want the whole bus to know!"

But it was too late.

"You're never going to guess who's calling George!" Amy shrieked at the top of her voice. "Dean Johnson!"

Everyone turned to look at George.

George knew that if she didn't answer her phone soon, her voice-mail would kick in.

She answered. "Hello?" George knew that everyone was looking at her. She tried to stay cool, but her heart was banging like a drum.

"Oh hi, Dean. Yeah, I'm fine thanks. You?"

George listened. Everyone watched George as she listened.

"Er, yeah, I'd love to!" she said.

Love to what? everyone thought.

"Yeah, that would be great!" said George.

What would be great? everyone thought.

"OK then. Cool. Yeah. Bye," George said before putting her phone away.

George looked out of the window. By now the bus was almost at school.

"Well?" Nick said. "What did he say?"

"Oh, nothing much."

"Nothing much? So why did he phone, then?" Nick asked.

"He just wanted to know if I'd like to go to the Cup Final, that's all."

"What?" Nick said. "You're kidding, aren't you?"

"No, Nick. I'm not kidding," George said.

"AAAAAAAGGGHHH!!!!" Amy screamed.

"What's happened? Who's died?" Denis asked, walking up from the back of the bus.

"Dean Johnson's asked your sister to go to the Cup Final with him!" Nick said.

"Well, not actually with him, because he's playing in it, isn't he?" said George. "But as a special guest, or something. I'm not sure, to be honest. He says he'll get back to me once he's talked to his agent."

"His agent? Why's he got to talk to his agent?" said Denis.

"I don't know," said George. "He didn't say."

"Right," Denis said. "And are you going to go?"

Nick and Amy looked at Denis as if he was mad. He obviously didn't realise what a huge deal this was.

"Well, I was supposed to be having coffee with Justin Bieber that day," George said. "But I can always cancel."

"Incredible, isn't it?" said Nick.

"Er, yeah, I suppose," said Denis. "If you like that kind of thing. Which I don't. But you know, each to their own and all that."

"Oh come on. You could at least try and be pleased for her," said Amy.

"Don't worry about it," said George. "He's always like that."

The bus slowed to a stop and the doors hissed open.

"Let's go," said Denis as he helped George down the steps and into the wheelchair. "How long now?"

"What? Till the Cup Final?" George asked.

"No. Till you get rid of this thing," Denis said.

"Oh, right," said George. "Dunno. End of the week maybe. Depends what Dr Patel says."

"Bet you can't wait, eh?"

"You're not kidding," said George.

"You won't forget, will you?" Denis added.

"Won't forget what?" said George.

"To phone Justin and cancel that coffee."

CHAPTER 9

PUSH OFF. NICK!

By lunchtime the whole school seemed to know. It was as if someone had made an announcement in Assembly. Everywhere George went, she was asked the same questions.

"Hey, George, can you get me a ticket?"

"Can you get me his autograph, George?"

"Can you give me his phone number?"

And everywhere she went, George gave the same reply.

"No."

"Why not?" one boy said.

"Because I haven't got a clue who you are," said George. "I've never even talked to you before. And now you're acting like we're best mates? What do you take me for? Some kind of idiot?"

"I was just ..." the boy began.

"You were just about to clear off," said George. "That's what you were just about to do."

The boy looked shocked. But at least he'd got the message. He walked away, leaving George and Nick alone.

"That was a bit harsh," said Nick. "He's just a kid."

"Yeah, a kid who's after something," said George. "Just like all the others. They didn't want to know me before."

"You can't blame them," Nick said.

George looked at Nick. "Pardon?"

"Erm, I mean you can't blame them for asking."

George thought for a moment. "No, I suppose not," she said.

Nick smiled. "Oh man, I can't wait," he said.

"For what?" asked George.

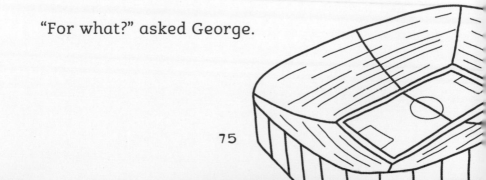

Nick looked at his friend. "You're kidding, right?" he said. "To go to the Cup Final? It's going to be amazing!"

George didn't say anything. She couldn't bring herself to look Nick in the eye. How could she tell him?

"What's up?" said Nick. "I am invited, aren't I?"

George shook her head.

"Seriously?" Nick asked.

"It's just me, Nick," said George. "Don't ask me why. I don't know."

"But I mean ... I thought ..." Nick looked like he was going to cry. "You'll need someone to help you."

"No, I won't," said George.

"What do you mean?"

"I'm going to be walking, by then. I won't need any help."

"Oh, right," said Nick. He sounded fed up. "I mean, that's brilliant about you walking, George," he added. "I'm dead happy for you. It's just that ..."

"It's OK, Nick, I understand," George said. "You don't need to explain. I feel bad about it as well."

Nick smiled again. It wasn't a huge smile. But it was a start.

"What?" George said.

"I think I know why he's only asked you," Nick said.

"Oh? And why's that then?" said George. But she knew very well what Nick was getting at.

"I think Dean likes you," Nick said.

"Don't be stupid, Nick!"

"Can I have a word please, George?" a voice boomed from down the corridor.

George didn't need to turn around. She knew who it was. It was Miss Parks, the head teacher.

"Is it about that little kid, Miss?" said George. "I can explain."

"Sorry?" Miss Parks said. "No, it's just that I've heard your news and ... well, I was wondering if you could get me Dean Johnson's autograph?"

Nick giggled. What would George say, this time? He doubted she'd tell Miss Parks to clear off!

"I'll do my best, Miss," said George.

"Thanks," said Miss Parks. "It's not for me. It's for my son. He's a big fan."

'Yeah right,' thought George.

CHAPTER 10

MAD WORLD

George's dad was so surprised, he almost spat out his coffee. "He's what?"

"Invited me to the Cup Final," George said.

"Whoa," said her dad.

It was later on that day. George should have been doing her homework, but she was watching TV instead. Her mind was racing, as she zapped between channels. She just couldn't think straight.

"Dean Johnson?" George's dad said, as if he still couldn't quite believe it.

"Yes, Dad. Dean Johnson."

"Invited you to the Cup Final?"

George nodded.

"Just you?"

"As far as I know, Dad. Yeah. Just me. Like a special guest or something. How mad is that?"

George's dad didn't reply. He had a faraway look on his face. It was either the look of someone who'd just won the Lottery, or someone who was desperate for the toilet. George couldn't quite decide which.

"Dad?" she said.

"What?"

"I said how mad is that?"

"It's er ... very mad, love. It's amazing!"

"I know," said George. "I can't quite get my head round it."

"I can't wait to tell the guys at work!"

George looked at her dad. He was so excited. He was like a kid who'd just been given the keys to a sweet shop. Which was a shame. Because George was about to snatch the keys back again. "Please don't tell the guys at work, Dad."

Her dad was puzzled. Why shouldn't he tell everyone? His very own daughter had been invited to the Cup Final! By Dean Johnson! It wasn't just a big deal. It was a massive deal! He wanted the whole world to know!

"Why not?" he asked.

"I don't know," said George. "I just don't want everyone to know, that's all."

"I don't understand," said her dad. "But, if that's what you want, love."

George smiled. "Thanks, Dad."

"Dinner's ready," called Denis from the kitchen.

"Great," said George. She stood up. It took a lot of effort. But she did it in the end.

"Are you sure you should be doing that?" George's dad said.

"I've got to practise, Dad," said George.

"But I thought Dr Patel said to take it easy."

"I've been taking it easy for the last two months!" said George. "I'm sick of taking it easy! I'm bored of taking it easy! It was just an operation! And anyway, Dr Patel's not here –?"

"Yeah but ..." Dad tried to say.

"No 'yeah buts', Dad," George shouted. "I'm walking and that's all there is to it. Now are you coming for dinner, or what?"

George's dad watched as George made her way to the door. He smiled to himself. He knew better than to argue with his daughter.

CHAPTER 11
READ ALL ABOUT IT!

"Have you heard George's news?" said George's dad, as he sat down.

"Yes, I've heard," said George's mum. "And I'm not very happy about it, either."

George's dad didn't understand. "Why not? It's incredible!"

"You think so?" said her mum, slamming a newspaper down on the table. "Have a look at this."

"DEANO CROSSES THE LINE!" screamed the headline, above a picture of an angry-looking Dean Johnson. Next to it there was another picture – of a very sweet-looking old lady.

"Read it," said George's mum. "Out loud. So we can all hear."

George's dad picked up the paper and began to read.

"Top soccer star, Dean Johnson, last night verbally abused an old lady in a supermarket car park. Foul-mouthed yob Johnson swore and raged at 83-year-old Vera Jenkins. And why? Because she'd taken his parking place. What makes this incident even more shocking is that it was a disabled person's parking place!

"'I couldn't believe it,' said Ms Jenkins. 'Some of the things he called me! I had to look them up in a dictionary when I got home. I was very upset. I'd only nipped out for a loaf of bread and some frozen peas. I'm not sure if I can ever face going to a supermarket again.'

"Asked whether she was sure it really was Dean Johnson, Ms Jenkins replied, 'Well, I'm not positive. But it looked like him.'

"Last night Dean Johnson was not available for comment."

George's dad put the paper down. Everyone turned to look at George.

"Well?" said her mum.

"Well what?" said George.

"Do you really think it's a good idea to be friends with this person? He seems a little ... What's the word I'm looking for?"

"Stupid?" said Denis.

"Mixed up," said George's mum.

"That's if you believe everything you read in the papers, Mum," George said.

"Fair point," said her dad. "And anyway how could he have sworn at an old lady last night? He was with George and Nick. Remember?"

George smiled. She was grateful to her dad for helping her out, but she could fight her own battles.

"Hmm, well. I'm still not sure it's a good idea," said George's mum.

"Yeah, and I still think he's stupid," said Denis.

"He is not stupid, Den!" George snapped. "He's just a bit ... confused."

"Whatever."

"No, Den," said George. "Not 'whatever'. I'm right. You're wrong. End of. And don't even think about saying 'whatever' again, OK?"

George glared at her brother, almost daring him. But Denis just smiled.

No one said anything for a while.

"What's he confused about?" George's mum asked.

"The whole fame thing," said George.

"Fame thing? What do you mean?"

"I mean he never wanted to be famous in the first place, Mum," George went on. "Being famous isn't easy, you know. It can be really tough. I don't think people realise that."

Denis pretended to sob. "Stop it, George. You'll have me in tears in a minute," he said.

"I knew you wouldn't understand," said George.

"You're dead right I don't understand," said Denis.

"Now, now, you two!" said George's mum. She looked to her husband. But George's dad appeared to be lost in thought.

"Dad?" said George.

"Yes?"

"What are you thinking?"

"Do you think he might have done it?"

"What?" George said. "You mean ..."

"Well, he might have done," said her dad. "You weren't with him *all* night."

George looked at her dad in amazement. "Don't tell me you think it's true!" she said.

"Erm, well ..." her dad began.

"I thought you were on my side, Dad!" said George.

But George's dad didn't get the chance to reply, because at that moment, George's phone rang.

"It's Dean," George said. "Would you like a word, Dad? You can ask him yourself. Go on. I dare you."

"Er, no, it's OK thanks."

"Hi, Dean, how are you?" said George. She stared at her dad. "A what?"

George paused.

"What for?"

Denis looked at his mum and dad. They all looked at George.

"Oh, right. I see. At your place?"

She paused.

"When?"

She paused again.

"Er, yeah, that should be OK. Great. See you then, Dean. Bye."

George ended the call. Everyone was still looking at her.

"Well?" George's mum said.

"There's going to be a photo-shoot," George said. "They want to take some pictures of me and Dean. I'm going to be in the papers!"

"Whoa!" George's dad said.

"Why?" George's mum said.

"Yeah, why?" Denis said.

"I dunno," George said. "His agent's organising it."

"His agent, eh?" Denis said, smiling. "That's interesting."

CHAPTER 12
NOT SO SPECIAL AGENT

The photo-shoot took place two days later, which also happened to be the day that George got to say goodbye to her wheelchair. Not that Dean Johnson's agent knew that, of course.

"OK, guys," Jeff Edwards said, in his best look-at-me-I'm-dead-important voice. "Before we begin, I'd like to have a quick word if I may."

A group of photographers was standing on the lawn in front of The Elms. A make-up artist was busy powdering Dean's face. She was like a thousand other young women Dean had met since he'd become famous. She flirted and fluttered her eyelashes and seemed to find everything he said completely hilarious. It was beginning to drive Dean mad.

That's why he was looking forward to seeing George again. He'd only met her that one time. He didn't really know her. But there was something about her. Something refreshing. Something a little bit different. Something a little bit ... normal.

"As you may know," Jeff went on, "Dean here has been getting some pretty bad press lately ..."

The photographers nodded and grunted in agreement.

"So we've asked you all here today, to show you that perhaps Dean isn't quite such a bad lad after all."

Jeff paused.

"We're expecting a guest to arrive any moment now. A very special guest. A very brave young lady and a good friend of Dean's. Her name's ..."

Jeff looked at Dean, who by now was trying on some different coloured shirts.

"What's her name again, Dean?" Jeff hissed.

"George," said Dean. "Her name's George!"

"George. Of course. How forgetful of me."

Jeff smiled before carrying on. "Now, George is going to be coming along to the Cup Final. As a special guest of Dean's. And we want as many people as possible to know about it. So what we're after is some nice photos of Dean and George. Happy, smiling photos that help capture the special friendship they have. Photos that show what a caring human being Dean Johnson really is."

Dean listened. Caring human being? Special friendship? What on earth was his agent on about?

"You know the score, guys," said Jeff Edwards. "You know what I'm saying here. We need a bit of good press for a change."

There were more grunts and nods from the photographers.

"Of course I wouldn't dream of trying to bribe you, but you're all welcome to stay behind afterwards. Have a look around. Relax. Maybe have a game of snooker, or a dip in the pool. Oh, and there's champagne. As well as a bite to –"

Jeff stopped. He'd seen two people walking across the lawn. One was a young guy. The other was a girl. Jeff thought she looked familiar. He'd seen her somewhere before. He just couldn't think where.

As they came closer, Jeff saw that the pair were walking arm in arm. The girl seemed a little unsteady on her feet.

"George!" called Dean. "Over here!"

Dean waved. The girl waved back.

"George?" Jeff Edwards said. "But ..."

"But what, Jeff?" Dean said.

"I thought she was ..."

"Thought she was what? Come on, Jeff. Spit it out!"

But for some reason Jeff Edwards couldn't spit it out. For once in his life he was lost for words.

"Hi," said George.

"Hi," said Dean.

"This is my brother, Denis," George went on.

"Pleased to meet you, Denis," said Dean.

"You too," Denis said.

"Hello. How are you?" George said to Dean's agent. "Or should I say, hell-oooooooo! How are yooooooooou?"

"Er, I'm fine thanks," said Jeff. "You're, er ... looking well."

"Never felt better!" George said with a big smile.

"That's good," Jeff said. "So, er ... where's your wheelchair, then?"

"What?" George said. "Oh, that thing? I don't need that any more."

"You don't?" asked Jeff, surprised.

"Why do you ask?" said Denis.

"Er, no reason," Jeff said. "Just wondered, that's all."

"Right," said Denis. He knew very well why Jeff had asked.

"Dean?" said Jeff. "Can I have a word please? In private?"

CHAPTER 13
THE FINAL COUNTDOWN

George slumped onto the sofa. She was worn out. It had taken a long time to walk back from The Elms. Walking again was taking a bit of getting used to, after all this time.

"How did it go, love?" her dad asked.

George looked at him. "It didn't," she said.

"What do you mean?" he said.

"The photo-shoot didn't happen, Dad."

"Why not?"

At that moment Denis came in with a glass of water for his sister. "I'll tell you why not," he said. "The only reason George was invited to the Cup Final was because she was in a flipping wheelchair!"

"What?" Mum said.

"They thought she was disabled," said Denis. "Well, Dean's agent did, anyway."

"Yeah," George said. "And as soon as he saw me walking, he couldn't wait to get rid of me. I mean the agent, not Dean."

"But Dean could've said something," said Denis. "But he didn't, did he? And do you know why? Because he didn't have the bottle!"

George was close to tears. Her mum sat down next to her on the sofa. "It's OK," she said, putting an arm around her daughter.

"It's not OK," Dad said. "It's a disgrace, that's what it is! How dare they? I've a good mind to –"

But he didn't finish. At that moment there was a loud revving noise outside. Denis went to the window. A bright red convertible Ferrari was parked in front of the house.

"Well, well," said Denis, as Dean Johnson got out of the car. "Talk of the devil."

"I'll deal with this," Dad said, getting up.

"No, please, Dad!" said George. "I can ..."

But it was too late. Dad had gone.

By the time George made it to the front door, her dad was already telling Dean Johnson what he had a good mind to do.

"George!" Dean said.

"How did you find out where I lived?" George asked.

"I bumped into your mate, Nick," Dean said. "He told me."

Dean paused. "Look, George, I just want you to know, that had nothing to do with me! Nothing at all! It was my people!"

George's face showed that she didn't believe him.

"I told you everything gets done for me. Remember?" Dean went on.

"Yeah, I remember."

"The photo-shoot was all fixed up. I didn't know a thing about it! You've got to believe me, George!"

"Yes, but why d'you think they asked me?" George spat out. "A girl in a wheelchair. They thought I'd make you look good! They were using me!"

"I didn't think of it like that," said Dean. "At the end of the day, I'm just a footballer. That's my job. That's what I'm paid to do!"

"Well, your agent was bang out of order," George's dad said.

"You mean my ex-agent," Dean said.

"What?" George said.

"I fired him."

"You fired him?" said George. "Just like that?"

"Yeah, just like that."

"Wow," said George. "Can you do that?"

"You're forgetting something," said Dean. "I'm Dean Johnson, footballing superstar. I can do what I want!"

Dean smiled. He wasn't being serious. George could see that. Her dad couldn't, though.

"In that case, any chance of another ticket for the Cup Final?" he said.

"No problem!" Dean laughed.

"Brilliant!" Dad said. "Thanks a lot, Dean!"

There was an awkward pause.

"We're not keeping you, are we, Dad?" said George.

"What?" George's dad looked at his daughter for a moment and then smiled. "Oh right, I see!" he said. "I'll, er ... leave you to it."

He went back in the house. George and Dean were left alone on the front step.

"I'm really sorry," Dean said.

"That's OK," George said.

Dean grinned. "You do still want to come, don't you?" he said. "To the Cup Final, I mean?"

"Are you kidding?" George said. "Of course I want to come!"

"Great," said Dean.

"Can I bring Nick as well?"

Dean smiled. "Course you can," he said.

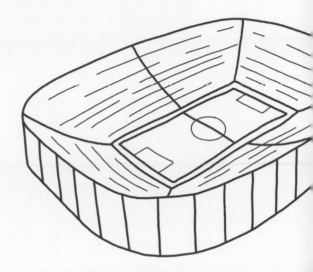

Our books are tested
for children and young people by
children and young people.

Thanks to everyone who consulted on
a manuscript for their time and effort in
helping us to make our books better
for our readers.